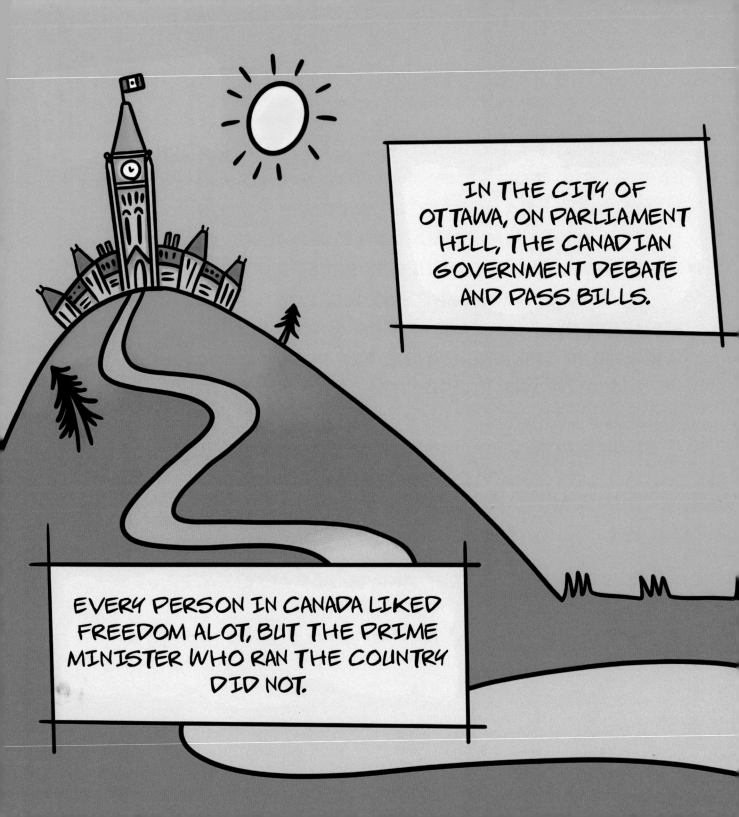

THE PRIME MINISTER HELD A CONFERENCE WITH EVERY NEWS STATION AS HE PITCHED HIS PLAN TO THE REST OF THE NATION.

THE PUBLIC OBEYED AND FOLLOWED THE RULES, 'TILL THE GOVERNMENT SHOWED THAT THEY TOOK THEM FOR FOOLS. SOME DIDN'T WEAR MASKS DURING THEIR CONVERSATIONS AND SOME EVEN WENT ON LAVISH VACATIONS.

FOR MONTHS THE FEDS HANDED OUT CASH AND DONATIONS WHICH TRIGGERED A BAD THING CALLED INFLATION.

FOOD PRICES SHOT UP AS
WAGES STAYED LOW AND ENERGY
COSTS CONTINUED TO GROW. AND
HOUSING IT BUBBLED, STUDENTS
COULDN'T MAKE RENT, SO THEY
CONTINUED TO LIVE IN THEIR
PARENTS BASEMENT.

I SIMPLY DON'T GET IT, I DON'T GET IT ONE BIT! THE TRUCKERS WON'T LEAVE, THEY CONTINUE TO SIT! THEY'VE BLOWN BOUNCY HOUSES AND BARBECUES IN THE STREETS. WHY WON'T THEY SIMPLY ADMIT DEFEAT? DANCE PARTIES, HORN HONKING, AS FLAGS WAVE TO AND FRO. THESE HORRIBLE TRUCKERS, THEY JUST HAVE TO GO!

AS THE DAYS WENT ON, IT CONTINUED TO GROW. AS THE PRIME MINISTER CURSED THEM AND SAID TO GO HOME. BUT THE TRUCKERS REFUSED, THEY CONTINUED TO STAND, FOR EVERYONE'S RIGHTS TO RETURN TO THE LAND.

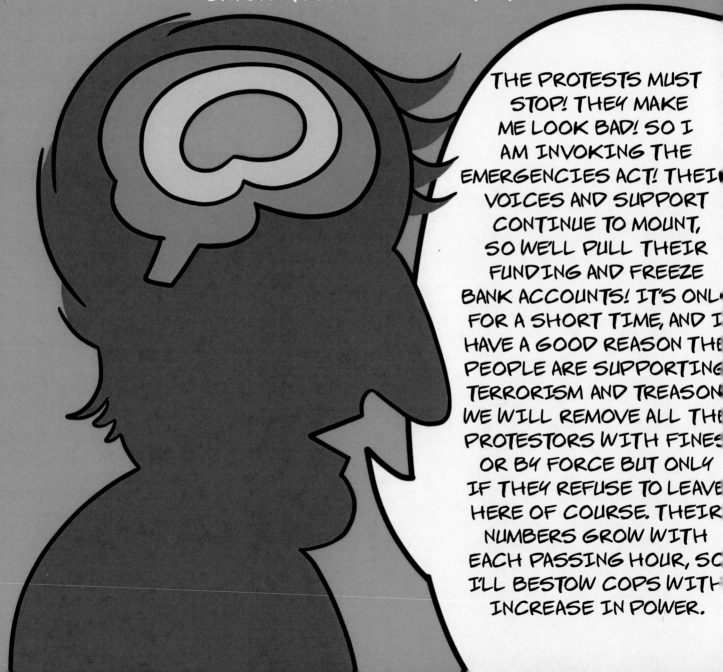

THE PRIME MINISTER JUMPED "YOU CAN'T DO THIS TO ME!" BUT THE MOTION WAS GRANTED AND ALLOWED TO PROCEED. THE VOTES CAME IN AND THE PRIME MINISTER WAS OUT, AS HE WAS ESCORTED OUTSIDE WHILE HE CONTINUED TO SHOUT.